Y0-BRM-731

CLOSED
FOR
DEMOLITION

To my children, Lauren, Evan, Michaela, and Mitchell, who loved going to the library for story time,
and to the tireless librarians who put magical possibilities into the hands of kids everywhere.
—Angie

To my ever-supportive family
—Rachel

Text Copyright © 2021 Angie Karcher
Illustration Copyright © 2021 Rachel Sanson
Design © 2021 Sleeping Bear Press

All rights reserved. No part of this book may be reproduced in any manner without the express
written consent of the publisher, except in the case of brief excerpts in critical reviews and articles.
All inquiries should be addressed to:

 SLEEPING BEAR PRESS™

2395 South Huron Parkway, Suite 200
Ann Arbor, MI 48104
www.sleepingbearpress.com
© Sleeping Bear Press

Printed and bound in the United States.
10 9 8 7 6 5 4 3 2 1

Library of Congress Cataloging-in-Publication Data
Names: Karcher, Angie, author. | Sanson, Rachel, illustrator.
Title: The Lady of the Library / written by Angie Karcher ; illustrated by Rachel Sanson.
Description: Ann Arbor, Michigan : Sleeping Bear Press, [2021] | Audience:
Ages 4-8. | Summary: Together a ghost and a girl make it their mission
to save the local library that is scheduled for demolition.
Identifiers: LCCN 2020031509 | ISBN 9781534111028 (hardcover)
Subjects: CYAC: Stories in rhyme. | Ghosts–Fiction. | Libraries–Fiction.
Classification: LCC PZ8.3.K1265 Lad 2021 | DDC [E]–dc23
LC record available at https://lccn.loc.gov/2020031509

THE LADY OF THE LIBRARY

ANGIE KARCHER

Illustrated by

RACHEL SANSON

CLOSED
FOR
DEMOLITION

Published by Sleeping Bear Press™

One roams the halls and walks through walls, then simply disappears.

The Lady of the Library has **haunted** here for years.

She floats
and flies
and flitters,
giving everyone a scare.

Each day she shrieks
and squeals, but now the place is bare.

Soon a few librarians box each and every book.
The Lady doesn't scare them. She sees how sad they look.

She swoops
        and sweeps—
a somber ghost in melancholy blue.

With no one left to frighten,
are her days of haunting through?

But then a little girl walks in, right through the grand front door.
She circles round the boxes that are stacked up on the floor.
She sits
and sketches
silently.
She knows just what to do. The little girl looks around.

"Hey, Lady . . . where arrrrre youuuu?"

The Lady is astonished, but she whimpers,
"I'm up here."

The girl holds out a tissue.
"Please, dismount the chandelier."

The Lady swooshes down,
        slowly
              swishes
                     with a swirl.

"We need to save this place!"
cries out the feisty little girl.

"Yes, I know! It's been my home for over eighty years."
They put their heads together as the Lady dries her tears.

They plot
    and plan,
        prepare
            as this crisis is extreme.

And this, their first attempt at a risky rescue scheme.

They stand up rows of books
to form a literary train.
And when the line of books
creates a long and winding chain,

they pack in paparazzi
and the press from far and wide.

Soon people come in droves to see this spectacle inside.

In hushed anticipation, people whisper as they lean
to get a peek of this mystique. A ghostly bookish scene.

The Lady gets it started
as the books fall
one
by
one.

The people cheer and donate
as they watch the falling fun.

The next day folks in hard hats are scattered far and near,
dismantling the reference desk and every bookshelf here.

The Lady screams
and squeals
and snickers.
The workers run in fear!

"Bwa-ha-ha-ha!"

she bellows.

"We don't want your sawdust here."

Soon the Lady and the little girl have hard hats on themselves.
They build a slide four cases high from all the wooden shelves.

They saw and sand until the slide is slippery and swift.
They polish, then they wax it to prevent a *splintered gift*.

The slide is luring people as they
hear the sander's humming.
They beg to see, to ride the slide,
and soon the crowds are coming.

The press and paparazzi come
from regions far and wide.

Townspeople come in
droves to see this spectacle inside.

The little girl is first to go. They count her down from
"Ten, nine, eight . . ."
and then . . .

she slips past science fiction, 201 to 304.
She zips past Chinese History and
slides by the Civil War.

The people give donations—the line is out the door—
and then they go around again to slide the slide once more.

They squeal,
they scream,
they smile,
until the last one gets to go.

The Lady and the little girl
hold boxes full of dough.

They count the dollar bills and change; it's simply not enough.
This mission seems impossible, too challenging, too tough.

Technicians shut off antique
lamps that light up every room.
Without the power, darkness fills
the place with midnight gloom.

The Lady's haunting outbursts
cause their mouths to open wide.

Their eyes are big as quarters
and their fear is hard to hide.
They stampede—scared—and stumble,
rushing quickly out the doors.

She proudly chuckles loudly,
"Don't come back here anymore!"

The Lady and the little girl both soon begin to pace,
not sure that what they've done will be enough to save this place.
They think
and think
and think, deciding one last thing to do.

A story time by candlelight will make its first debut!

They gather all the matches
found in drawers and storage places.
Then thirty-seven candles
light up the smiling faces.

They pack in paparazzi and the press from far and wide.
Townspeople rush back to see this spectacle inside.

The fire chief sounds the siren, his golden badge aglow.
"I see a fire hazard and I'm shutting down this show!

Your thirty-seven candles are a danger to the crowd."
He opens all the exits, shouting, "No flames will be allowed!"

The crowd begins to moan, and the Lady starts to sob.
The cheerful, joyful group is now a grouchy, grumpy mob.
The little girl says, "STOP!
STAY PUT!
I HAVE A SAFE SOLUTION!"

She raises up a box, illuminating resolution.

The Lady tells them chilling tales, shakes chains, then disappears.
She scares the people just a bit, as she has done for years.
She beams and blissfully bows as they beg for more and more.
Her Spooky Story Time keeps them coming through the door.

The mayor gives a sudden speech.
"I'll keep this nice and short. . . .
The library has been saved—
thanks for all of your support!"

The Lady gloats!
The girl, she gleams!
They glitter with delight.

The crowd then cheers 'cause now for years they'll have this lovely site.

The wooden floors still creak when there's no one in the room.
But now the Lady's happy—no longer filled with gloom.

She spooks them on the stairs, in the halls and lobby, too.
And maybe someday she will haunt a library near you!

Starlight Reading Room

Haunted Libraries

Do you believe in ghosts? How about haunted libraries?

Willard Library in Evansville, Indiana, is the oldest public library in the state and inspired this imaginary story. This historic haunted library was built and funded by Evansville millionaire Willard Carpenter in 1885. He was a huge supporter of education and felt that everyone should be able to improve themselves by learning. A public library would offer books and opportunities for everyone.

The famous ghost who supposedly haunts this Victorian Gothic building today is known as the Grey Lady. She was first seen in 1937 by a night custodian who was stoking the coal furnace. He reported that this lady ghost wore gray shoes and a gray veil. She disappeared when he dropped his flashlight. Soon after, he quit his job. The ghost is thought to be Willard Carpenter's youngest daughter, Louise. It is said she was upset when her father donated most of her inheritance to support the library. Fortunately, she seems to be a friendly ghost.

What are some of the Grey Lady's tricks? She turns water on and off in the restrooms and puts a chill in the air. She gently touches the hair or earrings of visitors, and she leaves odd items around the library. Often she makes loud noises, knocks books off shelves, and scoots furniture around. Visitors also say there is a scent of a strong perfume. Willard Library has been investigated by multiple paranormal groups and it even has a GhostCam that can be viewed online at any time of day.

It turns out that there are many haunted libraries across the country. Ghosts must love reading! It seems that most of these ghostly visitors are friendly. Paranormal experts feel that they may haunt libraries because this might have been a comfortable place where they visited or worked, they enjoy being around people, or it's a quiet, peaceful place. Many haunted libraries are very old historic buildings with lots of people passing through the doors over many years.

Not everyone believes in ghosts, but those who have experienced their presence are likely firm believers. How about your library? Do you think it would be a perfect place for ghosts?

Libraries Today

It's fun to think about haunted libraries, but the story within the story is that people need libraries! In the past, libraries housed books, newspapers, magazines, and other materials in print. Today, libraries offer far more than books. They have computers, free Internet, movies, classes, book clubs, music, audiobooks, e-books, and other electronic devices used for entertainment and learning.

Though funding for libraries varies from year to year and from place to place, people continue to support their local libraries. According to an article on the Libraries 2020 campaign website entitled "But, Nobody Uses Libraries Anymore!!" "more than 172 million Americans have library cards" and "libraries are visited over 1.3 billion times a year which is 10 times more than MLB (68 million), NFL (17 million), NBA (22 million), Hockey (21 million), and Nascar (4 million) combined."

Libraries are a great place to meet, learn, and celebrate with other readers in a community. The best ways to help keep your library thriving are to spend time there reading, participating in a class, watching a play, listening to an author or illustrator speak about their book, and celebrating whatever this public space brings to your community.

Do your part. Borrow books and lots of them. Take good care of them and return them when they're due. Make sure everyone knows how important the library is to you!

To learn more about the Willard Library, other haunted libraries, and what our public libraries have to offer, check out the articles and other resources below.

"10 Haunted Libraries of the US"
Open Education Database
https://oedb.org/ilibrarian/10-haunted-libraries-of-the-us/

Libraries 2020: "But, Nobody Uses Libraries Anymore!!"
https://www.libraries2020.org/but_nobody_uses_libraries_anymore

Willard Library
https://www.willard.lib.in.us/index.php

Willard Library Live GhostCams
http://www.willardghost.com/?content=ghostcams

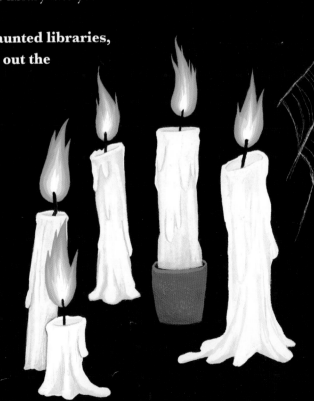